A Timeless Christmas: Stories from the 1950s to 1980s
Timeless Book Series book 1

James Holloway

ISBN: 978-3-1062-6420-0

Copyright © 2024 by James Holloway

All rights reserved.

No part of this book may be reproduced in any form or by any electronic or mechanical means, including information storage and retrieval systems, without written permission from the author, except for the use of brief quotations in a book review.

Contents

Foreword   v
About the Author: James Holloway   vii

1. The Silver Tinsel Tree (1950s)   1
2. Christmas by the Fire (1960s)   7
3. The Department Store Santa (1970s)   13
4. The Polaroid Picture (1980s)   19
5. Silent Night on Vinyl (1950s)   26
6. The Red Bike (1960s)   32
7. A Disco Christmas (1970s)   39
8. Home for the Holidays (1980s)   46
9. A Suburban Christmas Eve (1950s)   55
10. The Space Age Christmas Tree (1960s)   62

Closing Thoughts: A Timeless Christmas   69

Foreword

From the silver tinsel trees of post-war America to the flashing lights of a disco Christmas, these stories capture the essence of evolving family dynamics, societal changes, and the simple joys that bind us together, no matter the decade. Whether it's the sound of a crackling fire in the 1960s, a child's awe in meeting a department store Santa in the 1970s, or the instant joy of snapping a Polaroid picture in the 1980s, each tale evokes the tender feelings of Christmas past.

With stories that span the growth of suburban life, the rise of technology, and the changing rhythms of culture, this collection offers a heartfelt glimpse into the traditions and memories that made Christmas magical for generations. Whether you lived through these times or are simply longing to experience the charm of a bygone Christmas, this collection is a gift of nostalgia—a celebration of the timeless spirit of the holiday season.

Join us as we unwrap these heartwarming stories, each one a cherished memory from a Christmas long ago.

Foreword

About the Author: James Holloway

James Holloway is a master storyteller with a deep appreciation for the charm and simplicity of days gone by. Born in the early 1940s, Holloway grew up experiencing the post-war boom of the 1950s, the cultural shifts of the 1960s, and the vibrant energy of the 70s and 80s firsthand. His writing is often infused with a rich sense of nostalgia, capturing the everyday moments that define an era while celebrating the timeless themes of family, tradition, and wonder.

Holloway's ability to weave together historical details and emotional depth brings his stories to life, drawing readers into a world where the crackle of a vinyl record or the glow of a silver tinsel tree sparks vivid memories. He is known for his evocative prose and his knack for creating relatable, heartwarming characters that feel like old friends.

In *"A Timeless Christmas: Stories from the 1950s to 1980s,"* Holloway invites readers to take a step back in time, reliving the joy and magic of Christmas through the lens of four unforgettable decades. Whether it's the excitement of a child awaiting Santa or the quiet comfort of a family gathered around the fire, his stories remind us that while the world may change, the spirit of Christmas remains eternal.

When he's not writing, Holloway enjoys collecting vintage holiday memorabilia, listening to classic records, and spending time with his grandchildren, sharing stories of his own childhood Christmases.

Chapter 1
The Silver Tinsel Tree (1950s)

In the heart of the 1950s, a time when America was redefining itself, the world was awash with optimism. The streets of Maplewood, a small suburban town, reflected this spirit with neat rows of houses, each painted in pastel hues of blue, pink, and yellow. Smoke puffed from chimneys, filling the crisp December air with the scent of burning wood, and the windows of the houses glowed warmly with Christmas lights.

In one of these houses, at the end of a quiet cul-de-sac, lived the Sullivan family. Their small, modest home was like the others on the street—two stories, a white picket fence, and a backyard with a tire swing hanging from the largest tree. But this house had something else, something magical that only the Sullivans could feel: the spirit of Christmas.

INSIDE THE HOUSE, seven-year-old Maggie Sullivan sat cross-legged on the floor, carefully cutting out paper snowflakes with a pair of safety scissors. Every year, her mother would decorate the windows with the snowflakes, and Maggie was proud to be entrusted with the task. It was a tradition that filled her with joy. She hummed "Jingle Bells" as she worked, her dark brown curls bouncing with every snip.

"Maggie, don't forget to make enough for the front window!" her mother, Helen, called from the kitchen. The aroma of freshly baked gingerbread cookies filled the air.

"I won't, Mom!" Maggie replied, her voice filled with enthusiasm.

Helen peeked around the corner, smiling at her daughter's diligence. "And don't forget, we're putting up the new Christmas tree tonight. Your father's bringing it home after work."

Maggie's heart leaped. The Christmas tree! Every year, she and her father went to the lot down the street and picked out a fresh pine tree. It was one of her favorite parts of the holiday season, second only to opening presents on Christmas morning. She could already imagine the smell of pine filling the house, the needles soft and cool to the touch, the way it would look once decorated with their cherished family ornaments.

But this year was different. This year, there was no trip to the tree lot.

Instead, her father, Tom, had told her they were getting a new kind of tree, something she'd never seen before. "It's called a tinsel tree," he'd said with a twinkle in his eye. "It's shiny and silver, just like the ones you see in the fancy department stores."

Maggie wasn't sure what to think about that. A silver tree? It sounded strange, not at all like the trees she was used to. Would it still smell like Christmas? Would it feel like Christmas? She wasn't so sure.

As the hours passed, Maggie finished her snowflakes and helped her mother hang them in the front window, just as the first snowflakes of the evening began to fall outside. Helen stood back, admiring their work.

"They're perfect, sweetheart," she said, giving Maggie a kiss on the top of her head. "Now, let's clean up before your father gets home with the tree."

Maggie smiled, but her excitement was mixed with a little worry. She didn't want to upset her father, but she couldn't help feeling disappointed about not having a real tree. The thought nagged at her as she helped tidy the living room, arranging the sofa pillows and straightening the decorations on the mantel.

JUST AS SHE was fluffing the last pillow, she heard the familiar rumble of her father's car pulling into the driveway. Her heart began to race. She ran to the front door and flung it open just as her father climbed out of the car.

Tom Sullivan was a tall man with broad shoulders, the kind of man who looked serious at first glance but whose eyes sparkled with warmth and kindness. He was carrying a large, thin box, not the usual bundle of branches wrapped in twine that Maggie had come to expect.

"Daddy!" Maggie called, rushing down the steps to greet him.

"Well, there's my little elf!" Tom said with a grin. "Are you ready to see our brand-new Christmas tree?"

Maggie nodded, though her smile was a little shaky. "I guess so."

Tom noticed the hesitation in her voice and knelt down beside her, placing a hand on her shoulder. "It's going to be different, sweetheart. But different isn't always bad, right?"

Maggie looked into her father's eyes and nodded again, this time more confidently. "Right."

He kissed her forehead and stood up, carrying the box inside. "Okay, let's get this thing set up!"

INSIDE THE HOUSE, Tom set the box on the floor and opened it carefully. Maggie and Helen watched as he began to pull out pieces of the tree. The first thing Maggie noticed was that there were no branches, at least none like she had ever seen before. Instead, there were long, thin rods covered in shimmering silver tinsel. Tom attached them to a tall, metal pole that served as the tree's trunk.

When he was finished, Maggie stepped back and looked at the tree. It sparkled and shimmered in the light of the room, reflecting the glow of the fireplace and the soft twinkle of the Christmas lights her mother had strung across the windows.

"Well?" Tom asked, a little uncertainly. "What do you think?"

Maggie stared at the tree for a moment. It was strange, not like anything she had ever seen before. It didn't smell like pine, and it didn't look like the trees she was used to. But there was something beautiful about it, something magical. The way it caught the light and shimmered made it look like it was glowing from within, as if it were made of pure Christmas spirit.

"It's... it's pretty," Maggie said softly, her voice filled with wonder.

Tom smiled, relieved. "I thought you'd like it."

Helen clapped her hands together. "Now for the fun part—let's decorate it!"

They pulled out the boxes of ornaments, many of them passed down from Helen's and Tom's families. There were fragile glass balls painted with snowflakes, tiny wooden soldiers, and handmade angels. Maggie carefully hung each ornament on the tree, admiring the way they gleamed against the silver tinsel. The tree didn't need much to shine—it seemed to radiate light on its own.

When they were finished, Tom placed the final touch—a bright, golden star—on top of the tree. They stood back to admire their work, and Maggie couldn't help but feel proud. The tree was different, yes, but it was beautiful in its own way.

"It's perfect," Helen said, squeezing Tom's hand.

Maggie looked up at her father. "It's like something from a storybook."

Tom smiled and pulled her into a hug. "I'm glad you like it, sweetheart."

That night, after a dinner of hot soup and homemade bread, the Sullivans gathered in the living room. Tom sat in his favorite armchair with a newspaper, Helen busied herself knitting by the fire, and Maggie curled up on the sofa with a blanket. The tree twinkled in the corner, casting soft reflections across the room.

"Can we read a Christmas story tonight, Daddy?" Maggie asked, her voice sleepy but hopeful.

Tom folded his newspaper and smiled. "Of course. Which one?"

Maggie thought for a moment. "The one about the Christmas angel. You always read that one."

Tom nodded, reaching for the book that rested on the shelf beside his chair. It was an old, leather-bound volume of Christmas stories, its pages worn and soft from years of handling. He opened it to the story Maggie loved so much, and his deep, soothing voice filled the room as he began to read.

As Tom read about the angel who brought hope and joy to a small village on Christmas Eve, Maggie felt herself drifting off to sleep. The glow of the silver tree and the warmth of the fire made her feel safe, wrapped in the love of her family and the magic of the season.

Before she fell asleep completely, she whispered, "I love our tree, Daddy."

Tom looked over at his daughter, her eyes heavy with sleep, and smiled. "I love it too, sweetheart. Merry Christmas."

Maggie's last waking thought was of the tree, shimmering like stardust in the soft glow of the room. It was unlike any tree she had ever known, but it was theirs. And in that moment, as the snow fell softly outside and her family was gathered close, Maggie knew that Christmas was not about the tree itself, but about the love and memories that surrounded it.

And with that, she drifted into a peaceful sleep, dreaming of a Christmas that shimmered as brightly as their silver tinsel tree.

Chapter 2
Christmas by the Fire (1960s)

The snow fell gently outside, each flake dancing in the glow of the streetlights. The house on Chestnut Street stood tall and timeless, its windows frosted, warm light spilling onto the front lawn from within. It was Christmas Eve in 1967, and inside, three generations of the Thomas family had gathered for their annual celebration.

The smell of pine mingled with the rich aroma of baking pies and roasting turkey, filling the house with familiar comfort. In the living room, a large Christmas tree stood proudly, adorned with ornaments collected over the decades—glass baubles, hand-painted stars, and strings of tinsel that shimmered in the firelight. Stockings, some well-worn with age, were hung along the mantle, each carefully labeled with a name, from the youngest to the eldest.

THE FIRE CRACKLED in the stone hearth, its warmth spreading through the room, drawing everyone near. It was the centerpiece of their gathering—a fire that had burned for decades, lighting up Christmases past and present. The room was full of laughter, conversation, and the quiet hum of togetherness.

Seated in a large armchair near the fire was George Thomas, the patriarch of the family. His hair had long since turned silver, and his face was weathered with the lines of time, but his eyes still sparkled with life, reflecting the dancing flames. He held his youngest grandchild, four-year-old Emily, on his lap. She was captivated by the fire, her small hands clutching her doll while her eyes flickered between the flames and her grandfather.

"Grandpa, tell me a story," she said, her voice soft but eager.

George smiled, glancing around the room. His wife, Margaret, sat on the couch, knitting quietly as she had for so many Christmas Eves. Their daughter, Anne, and her husband, Frank, were busying themselves in the kitchen, preparing the last of the holiday feast. Anne and Frank's eldest son, Tom, now fourteen, was flipping through the latest issue of a comic book, while his sister, Maggie, twelve, perched on the rug by the tree, sorting through the presents.

"A story, you say?" George asked, leaning back in his chair. He rubbed his chin thoughtfully, the soft wool of his sweater brushing against Emily's cheek. "Well, let's see... How about I tell you the story of a Christmas long ago, when I was a boy?"

Emily's eyes widened, and even Maggie looked up from the presents. The room quieted as the rest of the family gathered closer, each person eager to hear George's story—a story they had heard before, but one that never lost its charm.

"It was the winter of 1921," George began, his voice low and warm. "I was just a little older than you, Emily. Our family lived on a small farm back then, and winters were hard. Snow would pile up so high that it seemed like the whole world had turned into a sea of white. But Christmas... oh, Christmas was always special."

. . .

THE ROOM GREW STILL as George's words painted a picture of the past. The fire crackled softly, as if keeping time with the story.

"We didn't have much, not like today," he continued, glancing at the tree and the presents piled beneath it. "But we had each other, and that was enough. On Christmas Eve, my father would gather us all around the fire, much like we're sitting here tonight. My mother would bake a pie—apple, if we were lucky—and we'd hang our stockings by the mantle. They were just old wool socks, but we'd hang them with care, hoping to find a few small treasures in the morning."

Emily nestled closer to her grandfather, her doll slipping from her lap as she listened intently. George's voice had a way of weaving the past with the present, making his memories feel alive and tangible.

"That particular Christmas," George continued, "we didn't have much in the way of gifts. The farm had struggled that year, and money was tight. But my father... he was a man of great spirit. He told us that Christmas wasn't about what was under the tree but about the love we shared, the stories we told, and the warmth of the fire on a cold winter's night. And you know, he was right."

GEORGE PAUSED, looking around the room at his family, all of them now gathered around the fire. His wife, Margaret, had put down her knitting and was watching him with a soft smile. Their daughter, Anne, had come in from the kitchen, wiping her hands on her apron, and sat down beside her children.

"That night," George said, "my father told us stories of his own childhood, of Christmases spent in a small village across the sea in Ireland. He talked of long, snowy walks to church, of carolers singing in the town square, and of the way the whole village would come together to celebrate. It was a simpler time, but it was full of magic. And that magic, he said, lived in the hearts of those who believed in the spirit of Christmas."

George's voice grew softer as he spoke of his father, a man long gone but never forgotten. The room seemed to glow with the warmth of the fire and the memories it evoked.

"We didn't wake up to a pile of presents that Christmas," George said, "but when we came down in the morning, we found something even better. My father had carved small wooden toys for each of us—just simple things, a horse for me, a doll for my sister—but they were made with love. And in our stockings, we found a few pieces of candy, a rare treat in those days. But what I remember most about that Christmas was the feeling of joy that filled the room. We sang songs, we laughed, and we held each other close. It was, perhaps, the best Christmas I ever had."

The room was silent for a moment as George's words settled over the family. Emily looked up at her grandfather with wide, wondering eyes.

"Was it really the best Christmas?" she asked, her voice small.

George smiled, pressing a gentle kiss to her forehead. "It was, my dear. Because it wasn't about what we had, but about who we were with. That's the real magic of Christmas."

Margaret, who had been listening quietly, nodded. "Your father always had a way with words," she said softly, her voice filled with affection. "He knew how to make the simplest moments feel extraordinary."

Anne smiled at her mother and father, her heart full of gratitude for the stories they had passed down over the years. She glanced at her own children, Tom and Maggie, who were listening intently, their usual teenage aloofness replaced by genuine interest.

"I think it's time we started a new tradition tonight," Anne said, standing up and walking over to the tree. She reached behind the tinsel-covered branches and pulled out a small box, wrapped in plain brown paper and tied with a red ribbon.

"This," she said, holding it up for everyone to see, "is a gift from all of us to you, Dad."

George looked surprised as Anne handed him the package. His hands, though steady, trembled slightly as he untied the ribbon and peeled back the paper. Inside was a beautifully carved wooden box, its surface polished and smooth, with intricate details etched into the wood.

"It's for you to keep your memories in," Anne said, her voice soft. "So you can pass them down to the next generation, just like you've always done with us."

George's eyes misted over as he opened the box. Inside were a few small items—an old photograph of his father, a letter Margaret had written to him when they were courting, and a tiny, hand-carved wooden horse, much like the one his father had made for him all those years ago.

"I don't know what to say," George murmured, his voice thick with emotion.

"You don't have to say anything, Dad," Anne said, kneeling beside him. "Just know that your stories, your love—they've shaped all of us. And now we want to keep them safe, for the future."

The fire crackled softly in the hearth, and for a moment, time seemed to stand still. Three generations of the Thomas family sat together by the fire, bound not by the gifts under the tree or the feast waiting in the kitchen, but by the stories they shared, the memories they cherished, and the love that filled their hearts.

Later that evening, after the presents had been opened, the food eaten, and the house quieted, George sat by the fire, the wooden box resting on his lap. Emily had fallen asleep in his arms, her tiny breaths soft and even.

. . .

He looked down at her peaceful face and then at the fire, the flames flickering gently. It was Christmas once again, and though the years had passed, the warmth of the fire and the love of his family remained constant, as steady and bright as ever.

"Yes," George whispered to himself, smiling as he held his granddaughter close. "This is the best Christmas."

Chapter 3
The Department Store Santa (1970s)

The air inside Watterson's Department Store was thick with the scent of pine needles, sugared gingerbread, and the faintest hint of freshly fallen snow. Outside, in the parking lot, cars were packed like sardines, their metallic bodies glinting under the soft winter sun. But inside, beneath the towering ceilings and twinkling lights, a world of Christmas magic unfolded. The year was 1974, and for eight-year-old Tommy Moore, this was the most exciting time of the year.

Tommy walked hand-in-hand with his mother, his small gloved fingers wrapped tightly around hers, barely able to keep up with her hurried pace. "Stay close, Tommy," she warned, her voice strained over the din of shoppers. It was the height of the holiday shopping season, and Watterson's was a madhouse. Every aisle was crammed with bustling families, hunting down the perfect gifts, their voices a chorus of holiday chatter. The floors shone underfoot, their polished surfaces reflecting the rainbow glow of multicolored Christmas lights that hung from every display window, archway, and shelf.

. . .

But Tommy had only one thing on his mind: Santa Claus. He could see the line of kids weaving through the toy department, stretching around towering stacks of board games, Easy-Bake Ovens, and gleaming Tonka trucks. At the end of that line sat the jolliest, most famous Santa in all of town, perched high in a golden, red-velvet throne. Every year, kids from all over made the trip to Watterson's for the chance to sit on this Santa's lap and whisper their Christmas wishes into his ear. The store's Santa was legendary—more than just a guy in a suit. There was something magical about him, something that made even the most skeptical kids believe.

Tommy tugged at his mom's hand, his heart beating fast with excitement. "Can we go see Santa now, Mom? Please?" His eyes sparkled as they darted towards the distant figure of Santa, a large man with a snowy white beard, his red suit shimmering under the store lights.

His mother smiled, a little tired but loving. "Alright, alright. Let's get in line," she said, and they joined the serpentine queue of children. Tommy was buzzing with excitement. He could hear the jingle of Christmas music playing faintly over the store speakers, "Silver Bells" drifting above the hum of voices.

As they waited, Tommy's gaze wandered, taking in the explosion of color and joy around him. The decorations at Watterson's were something special. Enormous candy canes hung from the ceiling, their red and white stripes twirling like something out of a dream. The windows were frosted with faux snow, where mechanical reindeer bobbed their heads and elves busily wrapped gifts with impossibly large bows. Christmas trees sparkled in every corner, their tinsel shimmering like threads of magic, and the air itself felt alive with a special energy. It was as if the store wasn't just selling Christmas—it *was* Christmas.

. . .

"Do you think Santa will know what I want?" Tommy asked, craning his neck to get a better look at the man in red up ahead. His mother kneeled down beside him, adjusting his woolen scarf and tucking a stray piece of his brown hair behind his ear.

"Of course, Tommy," she said softly. "Santa always knows."

They inched forward in the line, and Tommy's excitement built with every step. He looked around at the other kids, many of them dressed in their holiday best, girls in red velvet dresses with white collars, boys in neat sweaters and woolen trousers. Some looked nervous, clinging to their parents, while others were chatting excitedly, listing off toys they hoped to find under the tree.

Finally, Tommy was only a few kids away from Santa. The man himself looked perfect—his long, white beard as real as anything Tommy had ever seen, his red suit embroidered with gold thread that glistened in the light. His eyes twinkled with warmth and laughter, and every child that left his lap wore a smile brighter than the Christmas lights strung overhead.

When it was Tommy's turn, his heart raced as he approached the grand throne. Santa looked down at him, his smile widening. "Well, hello there, young man!" Santa's voice boomed like gentle thunder, deep and kind. "What's your name?"

Tommy felt a mixture of nervousness and excitement bubbling up inside him as he climbed onto Santa's lap. "I'm Tommy," he said, his voice a little shaky.

"Well, Tommy," Santa said, adjusting his red velvet hat, "have you been a good boy this year?"

Tommy nodded quickly, his face flushing. "I have! I promise!" He bit his lip, remembering the one time he broke his mom's favorite vase while playing with his toy truck. But surely Santa would understand. That was months ago.

"Good! Very good," Santa said, giving a wink. "Now, what would you like for Christmas?"

Tommy's eyes widened. This was the moment he had been waiting for. He leaned in close to Santa's ear, just like the other kids had done, and whispered his wish. "I want a G.I. Joe Adventure Team set. The one with the helicopter!"

Santa leaned back, a look of mock seriousness on his face. "A G.I. Joe Adventure Team set, huh? Well, I think we can manage that. You've been very good this year, after all." Santa winked again, and Tommy's heart leaped.

"Really?" Tommy's voice was filled with awe.

Santa chuckled, his belly shaking like a bowl full of jelly. "Really, really. Now, you keep being good for your mom, alright? And remember to go to bed early on Christmas Eve."

Tommy nodded eagerly as he climbed off Santa's lap. "Thank you, Santa!"

His mother was waiting just off to the side, smiling warmly. "Did you tell him what you wanted?"

Tommy nodded, his face glowing with joy. "He said I've been good, Mom! He said I might get it!"

She took his hand, her fingers gentle and warm, and led him through the crowd toward the exit. But Tommy wasn't ready to leave yet. The store was still brimming with magic, and he could feel it pulling him in every direction. His eyes darted toward the towering Christmas tree in the middle of the store, its branches heavy with ornaments and lights. Underneath it, kids were gathering around the toy train display that wound through the miniature village, with tiny houses dusted in white, and lamp posts glowing in soft yellow light.

"Can we go see the trains?" Tommy asked, tugging his mom's hand.

"Alright, but just for a minute," she said, a smile tugging at the corners of her lips.

They made their way to the display, where Tommy crouched down beside the track, watching in wonder as the train zipped past, its whistle blowing as it went. He imagined himself as the conductor, steering the train through snowy mountains and across vast, open plains, delivering toys to kids all over the world. The world of Watterson's felt endless, and in that moment, Tommy was no longer just a little boy in a department store—he was part of the magic.

As the train looped around again, something caught Tommy's eye. Over by the shoe department, there was a little glimmer, almost like a sparkle. He squinted, trying to make out what it was. It wasn't a decoration or a light, but something... someone. A small figure, dressed in green and red, scurrying between the racks of shoes.

Tommy's heart skipped a beat. Could it be...? An elf?

Without thinking, he let go of his mom's hand and darted toward the figure. "Tommy! Wait!" his mother called, but he was already weaving through the legs of shoppers, his eyes fixed on the tiny creature ahead. He followed the elf through the maze of displays, past the perfume counters, and into the men's department.

The elf darted behind a rack of coats, and Tommy, breathing hard, paused. He could hear the faint tinkling of bells, like sleigh bells on the wind. Slowly, he peered around the corner, his heart thudding in his chest.

. . .

AND THERE, in the corner, behind a row of suits, stood a small doorway—one Tommy had never noticed before. It was half-hidden by coats and scarves, but it was real. He could see the faint glow of Christmas lights from inside.

Taking a deep breath, Tommy stepped closer. The door was just his size. He crouched down and pushed it open, slipping inside.

He found himself in a room filled with twinkling lights and the soft hum of holiday music. Elves—real, living elves—were bustling about, wrapping presents, tying ribbons, and laughing as they worked. It was Santa's workshop, right here inside Watterson's.

TOMMY'S EYES grew wide as he took it all in. "This... this is real," he whispered, unable to believe his eyes.

One of the elves looked up and smiled at him. "You must be Tommy," she said, her voice like the sound of jingling bells. "Santa told us you might stop by."

Tommy could only nod, too stunned to speak.

"Well, you're just in time," the elf said, handing him a small, wrapped package. "A little something special for Christmas morning."

TOMMY LOOKED DOWN at the gift in his hands, his heart swelling with wonder. When he looked up again, the elf was gone, and the room had faded back into the familiar sight of the department store. His mother was there, her face a mixture of relief

Chapter 4
The Polaroid Picture (1980s)

The smell of pine needles and cinnamon filled the McAllister living room, mingling with the warm, sugary sweetness of cookies baking in the oven. Snow fell lightly outside the frosted window panes, gently blanketing the street, muffling the sounds of the neighborhood and adding to the sense of magic that hung in the air. It was Christmas Eve, 1986, and in the McAllister home, the holiday excitement was almost palpable.

TANGLED in the garlands that hugged the wooden banister, a string of colorful lights blinked erratically. The Christmas tree stood tall in the corner, adorned with ornaments the children had made over the years —popsicle stick stars, dough reindeer, and paper angels—each one telling a story, a frozen moment in time. But it wasn't just the tree that would capture the essence of this night. The family's old, trusty Polaroid camera rested on the coffee table, waiting to immortalize the night.

. . .

"Marty, hand me the stockings, will you?" Diane McAllister, a woman in her early forties but still radiating the youthful joy of the season, was busy perfecting the living room's decorations. She always took the lead in making the house look just right, ensuring that every detail was perfect for the big day.

Marty, her husband, was lounging in the worn armchair by the fire, dressed in a green sweater with a reindeer on it—an item he wore every year, regardless of how unfashionable it had become. He smiled and reached for the stockings, passing them to his wife. "You know, you could relax a bit, Di. It's all going to be perfect. It always is."

Diane laughed, a light, tinkling sound that danced in the air. "Not without a little effort! Besides, I just want to make sure everything is in place before the kids come back down."

"Speaking of kids," Marty said, leaning forward, "I think I hear them."

Thundering footsteps pounded down the stairs as three distinct voices filled the room. First came Danny, their sixteen-year-old son, taller now than Marty, with a mop of unruly brown hair and the hint of a mustache he was overly proud of. He sauntered into the room, hands stuffed in the pockets of his acid-wash jeans, looking nonchalantly cool but with a twinkle of excitement in his eyes.

Behind him, fourteen-year-old Kelly appeared, her wild, curly hair pulled back into a scrunchie, wearing a sweater that loudly declared, "Santa Rocks!" She was the family's social butterfly, always talking about boys, school gossip, and her favorite pop stars.

Then, trailing behind them with her stuffed rabbit clutched

under one arm, was little Emily, the baby of the family, just seven years old. Her wide blue eyes were brimming with anticipation, her hair still slightly damp from her bath, and she wore her favorite pink pajamas with little snowflakes all over them.

"THERE THEY ARE," Diane said, smiling wide at her children. "I was just telling your dad how this year's decorations look better than ever."

"They do, Mom," Kelly said with a grin. "And you know, I helped with the garland."

"Yes, you did," Diane agreed, patting Kelly on the back before turning her attention to Emily. "Are you excited for Santa tonight, sweetheart?"

EMILY NODDED VIGOROUSLY, her eyes darting toward the fireplace as if expecting the jolly man to tumble down at any moment. "Is it time for the picture yet?" she asked, her voice soft but insistent.

The family had a Christmas Eve tradition. Every year, just before the kids went to bed, they would gather in front of the tree for a picture with the Polaroid camera. It was a tradition that had started when Danny was a baby, and every year since, they had captured that one special moment: the five of them huddled together, smiling wide with the glow of the Christmas tree lighting up their faces. The photos always hung on the wall, a chronological display of the McAllister family's Christmases past.

"OF COURSE," Diane said. "We can't forget the picture. I've got the camera all ready."

Marty stood up and stretched, grabbing the Polaroid from the coffee table. "We've had this thing since before Kelly was born, you know," he said, shaking his head. "Still works like a charm."

"Because you take care of it like it's one of your own kids," Danny teased, smirking as he watched his dad carefully check the film inside.

Marty grinned. "Well, some things are worth keeping in good condition, aren't they?" He gave Danny a knowing look, which made the teen roll his eyes but smile nonetheless.

"All right," Diane said, clapping her hands together. "Everyone get in place! I want to make sure we get this just right."

Kelly pulled Emily toward the tree, and Danny followed, positioning himself on the other side of his younger sister. Diane joined them, standing beside Marty, who held the Polaroid at arm's length, ready to snap the shot.

"Okay, big smiles, everyone!" Marty called out. "On three! One... two... three!"

The flash went off, illuminating their faces with a bright, sudden burst of light. A soft whirring noise filled the air as the camera spit out the photo, still blank, waiting to develop.

Marty handed the square, white-framed picture to Diane, who smiled at it as it slowly began to show the outlines of their faces. "Look at that," she whispered. "Another perfect Christmas."

But as the image became clearer, Diane's smile faded slightly. The picture wasn't quite like the ones from previous years. There was something different about it—something intangible but present nonetheless. Maybe it was because Danny was taller now, standing on the edge, looking less like a boy and more like a young man. Or maybe it was the way Kelly's smile was more subdued, less carefree than in years past, with the faint shadow of adolescence casting a new layer of complexity over her expression. And then there was Emily, still the sweet, innocent child, but even she had grown in ways Diane hadn't fully noticed until now.

Time was passing. The kids were getting older, and the family, once a tight-knit unit, was starting to evolve. Diane could feel it in the space between them, the slight distance that hadn't been there before, the sense that their traditions, while still cherished, were changing too.

"Mom? You okay?" Kelly asked, noticing the faraway look on her mother's face.

Diane blinked and smiled, tucking the Polaroid into the pocket of her apron. "I'm fine, honey. Just... thinking about how much you kids have grown."

Danny rolled his eyes playfully. "Don't get all sentimental on us, Mom. It's just a picture."

"It's not just a picture," Marty said, his voice soft and warm. "It's a memory."

Danny shrugged, but he smiled too. "Yeah, I guess."

Emily yawned, leaning against her brother. "Can we go to bed now? I want Santa to come."

Diane laughed, the moment of nostalgia slipping away as she focused on the youngest of her children. "Yes, sweetheart, time for bed. The sooner you sleep, the sooner Santa will be here."

Marty took Emily's hand, leading her upstairs, while Diane stayed behind with Danny and Kelly, who lingered by the tree for a few more moments.

"You know, I'm kind of glad we do this picture thing every year," Kelly said softly, looking at the Polaroid camera still resting on the coffee table.

Danny nodded. "Yeah. It's cool to see how we've changed. Like, we're not the same kids we were when we started doing this."

Diane smiled at them both. "No, you're not. But that's okay. That's the way it's supposed to be."

AFTER TUCKING Emily into bed and making sure the stockings were filled, Marty and Diane finally had a moment to themselves in the living room. The fire crackled softly, and outside, the snow continued to fall, creating a peaceful stillness.

"You were quiet after we took the picture," Marty said, sitting beside his wife on the couch. "What were you thinking about?"

Diane sighed, resting her head on his shoulder. "Just how fast time is moving. Every year, it feels like the kids are growing up too quickly."

Marty wrapped an arm around her, pulling her close. "Yeah, they are. But we're still making these moments count, aren't we?"

She nodded, pulling the Polaroid from her pocket and looking at it again. The photo was fully developed now, the five of them standing in front of the tree, smiles wide and genuine. It was a perfect moment, frozen in time, even if time itself was moving faster than Diane would like.

"We are," she whispered. "And I'm glad we have this to remember it by."

THEY SAT TOGETHER in comfortable silence, watching the fire as it flickered and danced in the hearth. Above them, on the wall, hung the previous years' Polaroids, each one a snapshot of Christmases past—each one a piece of their family's history.

BUT THIS YEAR'S picture felt different, not just because the kids were older, but because Diane could sense the subtle shift in their family dynamic. Danny would be off to college soon, Kelly was already starting to talk about driving and high school dances, and Emily, sweet little Emily, wouldn't be the baby forever. The moments they had now were precious, and while they would always have the memories, Diane knew that nothing stayed the same forever.

Chapter 5
Silent Night on Vinyl (1950s)

C hristmas Eve, 1955
The first snowflakes of the evening began to fall, drifting like little tufts of down from a pillow burst in the sky. Outside, the streets of Maplewood Lane were cloaked in a thick blanket of white, and a quiet hush had settled over the small suburban neighborhood. Through the frost-laced window of a modest ranch house, warm yellow light spilled out, casting soft shadows onto the fresh snow. Inside, a fire crackled in the brick hearth, filling the room with the scent of woodsmoke and a cozy heat that mingled with the faint smell of pine from the Christmas tree standing proudly in the corner.

THE TREE WAS A FAMILY AFFAIR—DECORATED with tinsel and garlands, hand-painted ornaments, and strings of soft glowing lights. Beneath it, carefully wrapped presents were piled neatly, though not too high. Times weren't the easiest, but they were good enough. The family had what mattered most: each other.

. . .

A Timeless Christmas: Stories from the 1950s to 1980s

AT THE CENTER of the room sat a polished mahogany cabinet—the record player. Its elegant, curving edges and shiny brass fittings were the pride of the household. The year before, in 1954, it had been the big Christmas surprise from Richard to his wife, Eleanor. He had saved for months, setting aside a little from each paycheck from the mill, knowing how much she loved music. That record player was more than just a machine to spin discs; it had become the soundtrack of their evenings, the heartbeat of their home.

Now, Eleanor stood beside it, her fingers brushing lightly over the stack of records as she smiled to herself. She pulled out a worn sleeve and held it delicately, as though it were a treasure. It was a treasure. The faded gold lettering on the cover read, "Silent Night, Holy Night —The Choir of King's College."

IT HAD BEEN her mother's favorite. Eleanor could still see her, bustling around their old farmhouse, humming along as the record played from their own modest gramophone. This version of "Silent Night" had always been special to her mother, and now, it was Eleanor's favorite too. It was the song that brought Christmas into focus, that pulled the heartstrings taut with memories of past holidays, and of loved ones long gone. As she gently removed the record from its sleeve, she caught a whiff of that familiar old-paper smell, mixed with the faint aroma of worn vinyl. She held it with care, gingerly lowering it onto the turntable.

THE NEEDLE DROPPED with a soft *hiss*, and for a brief moment, the room filled with the sound of static. Then, slowly, the gentle opening notes of "Silent Night" began to play, the choir's voices rising softly, like the snow outside, enveloping the room in warmth.

. . .

From across the room, Richard looked up from his seat by the fire, his brow furrowing slightly as he glanced at his wife. He smiled. Eleanor had been quiet all evening, her mind clearly somewhere far away, but now, as the music filled the air, he saw her visibly relax. She sat down on the couch, folding her hands in her lap, her eyes distant.

"You alright, Ellie?" Richard asked softly.

She nodded, her eyes still on the record player. "Just thinking about home," she said, her voice barely above a whisper.

Richard understood. She always got this way around Christmas, ever since her parents had passed. It was hard to believe it had been nearly five years since she'd lost them both, just months apart. She'd been their only child, and now, all that was left were the memories, and the music that carried them back.

"Silent Night" played on, the notes curling around them, as though the very air in the room had become thicker, more intimate. There was a timelessness to it, a way it made the room feel both present and far away at once, as if the music bridged two worlds: the past and the now.

The front door creaked open, bringing with it a gust of cold wind and a flurry of snow. Tommy, their ten-year-old son, rushed inside, cheeks pink from the cold, a scarf wrapped clumsily around his neck.

"Tommy, close the door!" Eleanor called out, a smile breaking through her reverie.

He slammed it shut, stamping the snow from his boots before kicking them off in the entryway. "Sorry, Ma!" he said breathlessly. "It's really comin' down out there!"

Tommy bounded into the living room, eyes bright and eager as he spotted the record player. "Are we listening to the Christmas songs?"

he asked, eyes wide as the familiar strains of "Silent Night" washed over him. He flopped down on the floor near the fire, resting his chin in his hands as he listened, the way he had every Christmas Eve for as long as he could remember.

Eleanor smiled at her son, the sight of him like a balm for her soul. "Of course we are," she said. "It wouldn't be Christmas without it."

Outside, the snow was coming down heavier now, big, fat flakes piling up on the window ledges. The world beyond had turned into a snow globe, the streetlamps casting soft halos of light in the night. Inside, the warmth was almost tangible, wrapping itself around the family, tethering them to this moment.

As the last notes of the song faded away, Eleanor rose from the couch, making her way to the record player to start the song again. She didn't mind listening to it on repeat. In fact, it was a ritual of sorts —a way of keeping her mother's memory alive. Each time the choir sang, it was as though her mother was there in the room with her, just out of reach but still close enough to feel.

Suddenly, there was a knock at the door.

Richard and Eleanor exchanged a glance. "Who could that be, this late on Christmas Eve?" Eleanor wondered aloud, wiping her hands on her apron.

Richard stood up, lumbering toward the door with the ease of a man who had worked long hours and was grateful to finally be at rest. He opened it to reveal their neighbors, the Mortons, bundled up in heavy coats and scarves, their faces lit with excitement.

"Merry Christmas, Richard!" Mr. Morton said, his voice booming as he stomped snow from his boots. "We didn't want to intrude, but we're headed up to the church for the midnight service. Thought we'd see if you folks wanted to come along."

Richard hesitated, glancing back at Eleanor. "What do you think, Ellie?" he asked, though he already knew the answer. They'd planned on spending the night quietly, just the three of them. But something in the way Eleanor's eyes softened made him pause.

Eleanor stood by the record player, the needle poised over the start of "Silent Night" once again. She bit her lip, considering. The snow outside looked magical, the kind of snow that only comes on Christmas Eve, the kind that makes the world feel softer, more peaceful. Maybe it wouldn't hurt to go, just this once.

"We'll be along in a few minutes," Eleanor said, surprising even herself. She hadn't been to the midnight service in years—not since her parents had been alive. But tonight felt different. Maybe it was the music, or the snow, or the warmth of the room, but something inside her shifted. Tonight, she wanted to be part of something larger. She wanted to be in a place where voices could lift together in song, where the quiet of "Silent Night" could echo across the chapel and blend with others, creating something that reached beyond the walls of their little house.

Tommy jumped up from his spot by the fire, grabbing his coat excitedly. "Are we really going, Ma?" he asked, his face lighting up.

Eleanor smiled, nodding. "Yes, Tommy. We're really going."

As Richard helped her with her coat, Eleanor paused once more by the record player, her hand lingering over the dial. "Silent Night" had played so many times over the years, had been the soundtrack to so many Christmas Eves. The idea of leaving it behind for the evening felt strange, but she knew the music wasn't just on the vinyl. It was in her heart, and in the memory of her mother.

The three of them bundled up and stepped out into the night, the snow crunching beneath their boots as they made their way down the street toward the little church on the hill. The Mortons waved from up ahead, their laughter and chatter floating back on the cold air.

As they walked, Eleanor could still hear the music in her mind, the soft strains of "Silent Night" that had filled the house moments before. But now, as they approached the church and the glow of the windows, she realized that the song was everywhere. It was in the snowflakes, in the quiet peace of the night, and in the warmth of her family walking beside her.

When they reached the church, they stepped inside, greeted by the scent of pine and candlewax. The congregation was already gathering, the choir warming up. And as they took their seats, Eleanor closed her eyes, feeling the music rise around her, wrapping her in the comfort of Christmas, of home, of love.

And when the choir began to sing "Silent Night," the sound swelled and soared, filling the old chapel with a grace that transcended the years. Eleanor let herself be carried away, not just by the music, but by the memories, by the promise of peace, and by the enduring magic of Christmas Eve.

As the final note hung in the air, Eleanor smiled to herself. Tonight, the music wasn't just a memory. It was alive, here and now, and always would be.

Chapter 6
The Red Bike (1960s)

It was the winter of 1964, and the small suburban town of Maplewood was wrapped in a layer of fresh snow. Christmas lights twinkled on the houses lining the streets, and the scent of pine and fresh-baked cookies filled the air. The town, like many in the growing suburbs of America, had sprung up in the post-war boom. Rows of modest homes stood proudly on neat streets, each one filled with the aspirations of families chasing the American Dream. Among them was the Thompson family, living in a pale blue ranch-style house at the end of Oak Street. It was the kind of place where kids played stickball in the summer and sledded down neighborhood hills in the winter, where the world felt safe and full of possibility.

For ten-year-old Tommy Thompson, Christmas that year meant only one thing: the red bike. It was all he could think about, dream about, talk about. The Schwinn Sting-Ray was the latest craze, and this one, with its bright red frame, banana seat, and high-rise handlebars, was the stuff of legend. Tommy had seen it in the window of Meyer's Hardware Store downtown every day for the past month. It gleamed like a beacon of hope and adventure, calling out to him with promises of freedom and fun.

Every day after school, Tommy would race over to Meyer's just to look at it. The old shopkeeper, Mr. Meyer, was used to seeing Tommy press his nose against the glass, his breath fogging up the window as he gazed longingly at the bike. Mr. Meyer, with his bushy white mustache and kind eyes, would often wave at Tommy and chuckle to himself, knowing well the look of a boy who had fallen in love with something so out of reach.

Tommy knew the bike was expensive. He'd overheard his parents talking about money more than once, especially after his dad lost his job at the factory in the spring. Dad had found work again, but it was a long drive into the city, and there were always whispers between his parents at night, the kind of quiet conversations that ended with deep sighs and worried glances. Still, Tommy couldn't help but hope. He had been extra good this year, helping his mom with chores and keeping his grades up at school. Maybe, just maybe, if he wished hard enough, Santa might bring him the red bike.

One crisp afternoon, about a week before Christmas, Tommy stood outside Meyer's once more, staring at the bike. Snowflakes drifted down lazily from the sky, landing softly on his woolen cap. He imagined himself riding down the hill near his house, the wind whipping through his hair, the world rushing by in a blur. He could see himself racing past the other kids, who would watch in envy as he sped by on the coolest bike in the neighborhood.

. . .

"Thinking about the bike again, huh?" a voice interrupted his daydream.

Tommy turned to see his friend, Billy Jenkins, standing beside him. Billy lived two streets over and was in Tommy's class at school. He was taller than Tommy and had a shock of unruly blonde hair that stuck out from under his knit hat.

"Yeah," Tommy said with a sigh. "It's the best bike I've ever seen."

Billy grinned. "My dad says it's too expensive. Says I'll have to wait until my birthday if I want one."

"Mine, too," Tommy admitted. "But I can't stop thinking about it. Do you think Santa might bring it?"

Billy shrugged. "Maybe. My mom says Santa can't do everything. But I figure if anyone can, it's him."

Tommy nodded, though a small pit of doubt settled in his stomach. He wanted to believe in Santa, but as he got older, it was becoming harder to hold onto that childlike faith. His older sister, Judy, had told him last year that Santa wasn't real, but Tommy refused to believe her. If Santa wasn't real, who else would bring him the red bike?

The boys stood in silence for a moment, staring at the bike through the frosted glass. It seemed to shimmer under the soft glow of the shop's Christmas lights, as if it knew it was the object of their deepest desire.

"I'll race you home," Billy said suddenly, breaking the spell.

Tommy smiled. "You're on."

They took off running through the snow-covered streets, their boots crunching against the frozen ground, their breath visible in the cold air. The town of Maplewood felt alive with Christmas cheer—houses decorated with twinkling lights, wreaths hanging on doors, the occasional sound of carolers singing in the distance. As Tommy ran, his heart lightened. Maybe, just maybe, this Christmas would be the one he'd always dreamed of.

CHRISTMAS EVE ARRIVED, and the Thompson household buzzed with excitement. The smell of roasting turkey wafted through the air, and the Christmas tree stood proudly in the living room, adorned with tinsel and colorful ornaments. Tommy's parents had been busy all day, preparing for the small gathering they were hosting that evening. Tommy's grandparents were coming over, along with his Uncle Joe and Aunt Marcy. It was tradition to have a big family dinner on Christmas Eve, followed by hot cocoa and opening one present before bed.

TOMMY COULDN'T STOP THINKING about the red bike. All day long, he'd tried to catch a glimpse of anything resembling a large, bike-shaped package hidden somewhere in the house, but there was nothing. His dad had brought in a few wrapped gifts from the car earlier, but none of them looked big enough to be a bike. Still, Tommy clung to hope.

That evening, as the family gathered around the table for dinner, Tommy found it hard to concentrate. His mind was elsewhere, imagining what it would be like to wake up in the morning and find the red bike under the tree. He could hardly sit still through dinner, and when it was finally time to open one present, he tore into his with barely contained excitement.

INSIDE WAS A WOOLEN SCARF, hand-knitted by his grandmother.

Tommy tried to hide his disappointment, forcing a smile as he thanked her. The scarf was nice, but it wasn't the red bike.

That night, after everyone had gone home and the house was

quiet, Tommy lay in bed, staring up at the ceiling. He could hear the faint sound of his parents talking downstairs, but he couldn't make out what they were saying. His heart ached with worry. What if there was no red bike? What if Santa didn't come through this year?

As sleep finally overtook him, Tommy dreamed of the bike, its red frame shining in the sunlight, the wheels spinning as he rode down the street faster than the wind.

CHRISTMAS MORNING DAWNED bright and cold. Sunlight streamed through the curtains in Tommy's room, and he woke with a start, his heart pounding in anticipation. This was it—the moment he had been waiting for. He jumped out of bed, barely taking the time to put on his robe before racing downstairs.

THE LIVING ROOM was filled with gifts—brightly wrapped packages piled high under the tree. Tommy's parents were already there, sitting on the couch with steaming mugs of coffee in their hands. His sister Judy was there, too, still rubbing the sleep from her eyes.

"Merry Christmas!" his mom said with a smile as Tommy skidded to a stop in front of the tree.

"Merry Christmas!" Tommy replied breathlessly, his eyes scanning the room for any sign of the bike.

There was no red bike in sight.

HIS HEART SANK, but he tried to hide his disappointment. Maybe it was hidden somewhere else in the house. Maybe it would be the last gift he opened, saved for the grand finale.

They began opening presents, and one by one, Tommy's pile of gifts grew smaller. There were clothes, books, and a few toys, but no red bike. Finally, there was only one gift left—a small box, wrapped in shiny red paper. It was from his parents.

Tommy tore off the wrapping and opened the box, his heart racing. Inside was a folded piece of paper. Confused, he pulled it out and read the words written in his dad's familiar handwriting:

Go to the garage.

Tommy's eyes widened. Without a second thought, he bolted for the door, his family laughing behind him. He threw open the door to the garage, and there, in the middle of the floor, was the red bike. It was even more beautiful than he had imagined. The bright red paint gleamed in the morning light, the chrome handlebars shining like silver. A red bow was tied around the frame, and it looked like something out of a dream.

For a moment, Tommy just stood there, staring at the bike in disbelief. Then, with a shout of joy, he ran over to it, running his hands along the smooth frame. It was real. It was his.

"Merry Christmas, Tommy," his dad said from the doorway, his voice filled with warmth.

Tommy turned, his eyes shining with happiness. "Thank you! Thank you so much!"

His dad smiled, ruffling Tommy's hair. "You've been a good kid this year. You deserve it."

Tommy climbed onto the bike, gripping the handlebars and imagining all the adventures he would have. In that moment, the world felt perfect. All his doubts and worries melted away, replaced by the pure joy of childhood dreams come true.

As he rode the bike out of the garage and into the snowy streets of Maplewood, the wind whipping through his hair, Tommy knew he would never forget this Christmas—the Christmas of the red bike, when dreams became reality and the magic of the season filled his heart.

Chapter 7
A Disco Christmas (1970s)

The air outside was crisp, the kind of sharp cold that bit through your polyester bell-bottoms and filled your lungs with a stinging sensation. The night had that magical quality that only comes around during the holiday season—a certain stillness that made you want to wrap yourself in layers of scarves and mittens and bask in the glow of colored Christmas lights hanging on every street corner. It was December 1978, and everywhere you looked, the world shimmered with the kind of energy that made you feel anything was possible. And nowhere was that energy more alive than at *Starshine Disco*.

INSIDE STARSHINE, the night was just beginning. It was a place where people came not just to dance, but to lose themselves in the rhythm of the music, to find something they couldn't name in the blur of flashing lights and pounding bass lines. The disco was housed in a once grand theater, now repurposed into the hottest club in town. The arched ceiling was studded with thousands of tiny mirrors, catching the reflections of the multi-colored strobe lights that bounced off the dance floor below. At the center of it all, suspended high above the crowd, was a massive spinning disco ball, casting speckles of light in every direction like a sky full of stars.

TONIGHT, though, wasn't just any night at *Starshine*. It was Christmas Eve, and the disco had transformed into a winter wonderland—70s style, of course. Giant plastic candy canes leaned against the DJ booth, silver tinsel lined the walls, and a floor-to-ceiling artificial Christmas tree glistened with gaudy ornaments and flashing lights. The scent of cinnamon and pine filled the air, mixing with the distinct aroma of vinyl and cigarette smoke. It was as if the whole place had been dipped in glitter and wrapped in a red velvet bow.

MIA STOOD BY THE ENTRANCE, adjusting the straps of her platform sandals. Her afro, perfectly picked out, framed her face like a halo, and her glittery gold jumpsuit caught the light in a way that made her look like she was glowing. She was twenty-two, working as a secretary by day, but by night she was a regular at *Starshine*, where she could forget the monotony of her 9-to-5 job and let the music take over. She smiled as she surveyed the crowd that was slowly gathering. Everyone seemed to be on the same wavelength tonight—ready to dance, ready to celebrate, ready to let loose.

HER BEST FRIEND, Tony, was supposed to meet her here any minute. Tony was the one who had first introduced her to disco, dragging her to *Starshine* one Saturday night two years ago when she was still too shy to even sway in her seat. Now, Mia was known for being the first one on the dance floor, her moves smooth and effortless as she twirled and spun, her arms lifted high to catch the rhythm. Disco had a way of getting under your skin like that—it was infectious, impossible to resist.

. . .

As she scanned the room, the familiar strains of Gloria Gaynor's "I Will Survive" started to pulse through the speakers, and Mia couldn't help but grin. It was like the anthem of the era, a song that made you feel invincible. She swayed to the beat, her hips moving in time with the music, when she spotted Tony weaving through the crowd toward her. He was impossible to miss, with his tight white bell-bottoms and a purple silk shirt that billowed as he moved, his hair slicked back in a perfect pompadour.

"Merry Christmas, disco queen!" Tony shouted over the music, pulling her into a tight hug.

"Merry Christmas, Tony!" Mia laughed, giving him a playful shove. "You look like you just stepped out of a Bee Gees video."

"You know I have to bring the sparkle tonight," he said with a wink, twirling once to show off his outfit. "Besides, it's Christmas Eve. Gotta make it count!"

They made their way toward the dance floor, already buzzing with people, some wearing Santa hats with sequins, others draped in tinsel as if it were the most natural accessory in the world. The DJ, a guy who called himself DJ Ice, was in the booth, his headphones perched atop his head as he worked the turntables, seamlessly blending from one track to the next.

"Come on, Mia, let's show these people how it's done," Tony said, grabbing her hand and pulling her to the center of the floor.

The music shifted to "Don't Leave Me This Way" by Thelma Houston, and in an instant, Mia felt the familiar warmth of the beat wrap around her. The sound was deep, resonant, and irresistible. She closed her eyes for a moment, letting the bass line thump in her chest, the strings soaring over it like waves crashing against a shore. When she opened her eyes, Tony was already moving, his arms stretched wide as he swayed to the rhythm.

THEY DANCED TOGETHER, lost in the groove, their movements perfectly in sync. Around them, people were clapping, spinning, and laughing, the energy building with each passing second. It wasn't long before Mia felt the sweat start to bead on her forehead, but she didn't care. This was where she was meant to be—on the dance floor, surrounded by people who felt the music as deeply as she did. The disco was more than just a place to dance; it was a community, a home away from home, especially on nights like this when the outside world felt cold and distant.

AFTER WHAT FELT LIKE HOURS, Mia and Tony finally took a break, collapsing into one of the plush velvet booths that lined the back wall. A waitress in a red miniskirt and knee-high boots brought them two glasses of champagne, courtesy of the club owner, who was in an exceptionally generous mood tonight.

"Cheers to another year of dancing our hearts out," Tony said, raising his glass. "And to the best disco partner in town."

Mia clinked her glass against his. "And to you, Tony, for always making sure I never miss a beat."

THEY SIPPED THEIR CHAMPAGNE, the bubbles tickling their noses, and for a moment, the world outside the disco felt miles away. The weight of daily life—work, bills, the uncertainties of the future—vanished, replaced by the simple joy of the present moment.

Suddenly, the lights dimmed, and the music faded, leaving only a faint hum in the background. Mia looked up, confused. The dance floor, once full of bodies in motion, was now still, the crowd murmuring in surprise. Then, from the back of the club, a spotlight appeared, casting its beam on the DJ booth, where DJ Ice was now standing with a microphone in hand.

"Ladies and gentlemen," he began, his voice smooth and cool. "Tonight is a special night, not just because it's Christmas Eve, but because we've got a little surprise for you."

Mia glanced at Tony, who shrugged, just as curious as she was. The crowd buzzed with anticipation, and Mia could feel her heart race in excitement.

DJ Ice paused for dramatic effect, then pointed toward the entrance. "Please welcome...Santa Claus!"

The crowd erupted into laughter and applause as a figure dressed in a red velvet Santa suit, complete with a white beard and black boots, strutted onto the dance floor. But this wasn't your typical mall Santa. No, this Santa had swagger. He walked with the confidence of someone who knew how to command a room, his movements exaggerated and playful. The crowd parted as he made his way to the center of the dance floor, and when he reached the middle, he spun around and whipped off his Santa hat, revealing a head full of curly hair.

"Oh my God," Mia gasped, recognizing him instantly. "Is that...?"

"Is that Isaac Hayes?" Tony finished for her, his mouth hanging open.

Sure enough, Isaac Hayes, the legendary soul singer, stood in the center of *Starshine Disco*, dressed as Santa Claus and grinning from ear to ear. The crowd went wild, and Mia found herself screaming in excitement along with everyone else.

Hayes raised his hands, quieting the crowd, and the DJ cued up a familiar beat—the opening bars of Hayes' classic "Theme from Shaft." The room exploded with energy as the song kicked in, the funky bass line and sharp horns filling the air. Hayes, still in his Santa suit, began to dance, his moves smooth and effortless, as if the Santa costume were just an extension of his soul.

MIA COULDN'T BELIEVE what she was seeing. Isaac Hayes—Isaac Hayes!—dancing right there in front of her, in a disco on Christmas Eve. It was like a dream, one of those surreal moments that didn't quite seem real, but there he was, larger than life, leading the entire club in an impromptu dance party.

Tony grabbed Mia's hand, and they rushed back to the dance floor, joining the throng of people who were now grooving to the music with wild abandon. The Christmas tree lights blinked in time with the beat, the disco ball spinning overhead, casting a million tiny reflections across the room. It was chaos and joy, a whirlwind of movement and sound that made everything else fade away.

FOR THE NEXT FEW HOURS, the party at *Starshine* reached new heights. Isaac Hayes performed a few more songs, mixing his soulful voice with the infectious disco beats, and by the time he finally left the stage—after promising to return next year—the crowd was riding a high that only music could bring.

As the night wore on, Mia and Tony found themselves back in their booth, breathless and exhilarated, their cheeks flushed from dancing. The clock had long since struck midnight, and it was now officially Christmas Day.

"MERRY CHRISTMAS, MIA," Tony said, leaning back in his seat, his eyes twinkling.

"Merry Christmas, Tony," Mia replied, her heart full. "This...this is one for the books."

They sat in comfortable silence for a moment, watching the last of the dancers on the floor, the disco lights still spinning, the music still pulsing softly in the background. It was a night they would never forget—a night where the magic of Christmas and the power of disco had come together in a way that could only happen in the 1970s.

AND AS THEY left *Starshine* in the early hours of Christmas morning, the city streets quiet and blanketed in a light dusting of snow, Mia couldn't help but smile. Disco, she thought, was the gift that kept on giving.

And tonight, it had given her the best Christmas of her life.

Chapter 8
Home for the Holidays
(1980s)

December 1987. The sky was a deep, inky black, sprinkled with stars that twinkled like tiny lights hung above the sleepy town of Willow Creek. It was a small, unremarkable place, the kind of town you either left as soon as you were old enough or stayed in for the rest of your life. But for one family, it was home. And it was Christmas.

THE TAYLOR HOUSE sat on a quiet street lined with snow-covered oaks. A gentle breeze stirred the branches, sending powdery flurries onto the pavement below. The house itself was a vision of holiday cheer, draped in glowing red and green lights that reflected off the layer of snow covering the roof. In the window, a Christmas tree sparkled with tinsel, handmade ornaments, and the warm glow of colored bulbs.

INSIDE, the scent of cinnamon and pine filled the air. Gloria Taylor moved about the kitchen with the ease of a conductor leading a symphony. The oven timer dinged, and she pulled out a tray of sugar cookies, the edges browned just the right amount, each one shaped like snowmen, reindeer, and Christmas trees. She set the tray down on the counter and turned to stir the pot of hot cocoa on the stove.

It was the Saturday before Christmas, and for the first time in years, all of her children were coming home.

As she worked, Gloria's thoughts wandered back through the years. It seemed like only yesterday when her kids were small, running through the halls of this house, squabbling over toys, and filling the rooms with laughter. But now they were all grown up, scattered across the country. Life had taken them in different directions, each one chasing their own dreams. There was hardly time to be a family anymore. But for this one holiday, for this one moment, they would all be under the same roof again.

She reached for a small picture frame on the kitchen counter. It was from Christmas 1979, the last time they were all together, when the kids were still young. In the photo, her eldest, Danny, was holding up a new Walkman, grinning from ear to ear. Next to him was his younger brother, Mark, caught mid-laugh as he tried on a ridiculous sweater Gloria had knitted for him. Sarah, the baby of the family, was holding a Cabbage Patch Kid doll with a look of pure delight.

Now, Danny was thirty-two and living in New York City, a high-powered advertising executive with little time to even call home. Mark was thirty, a musician who had spent most of the last five years on the road, playing in smoky bars and clubs. And Sarah, now twenty-six, was an assistant manager at a department store in Chicago, climbing her way up the corporate ladder.

. . .

It had been so long since they'd all been together for Christmas. Gloria worried that time and distance had changed them—that the bond they once shared had frayed. But she was determined to bring that sense of family back, if only for a few days.

The clock on the wall ticked closer to 6:30, the time they were all supposed to arrive. Gloria wiped her hands on her apron and walked to the living room. Her husband, Frank, sat in his favorite armchair, reading the paper. He looked up and smiled.

"Everything ready?" he asked, folding the paper and setting it aside.

"As ready as it'll ever be," Gloria said with a sigh. "Do you think they'll be on time?"

Frank chuckled. "It's Christmas. They'll be here."

She nodded, trying to quell the anxious flutter in her chest. Frank had always been the calm one, the steady rock in their family. He'd been retired for a few years now, after a long career at the steel mill. In many ways, he hadn't changed much—he still wore his plaid flannel shirts and blue jeans, still had that same comforting presence. But Gloria could see the age creeping up on him, in the deepening lines around his eyes and the way his hair had turned from brown to white seemingly overnight.

They both sat in comfortable silence, the sound of a cassette tape playing softly in the background. It was one of Frank's favorites—Simon & Garfunkel, their voices smooth and harmonious, perfect for a snowy December evening.

The silence was interrupted by the sound of tires crunching on the snow outside. Gloria jumped up, her heart skipping a beat. She rushed to the window and peered out into the night.

. . .

A BLUE PONTIAC pulled up in the driveway, the headlights cutting through the darkness. The driver's side door opened, and out stepped Danny, tall and broad-shouldered in his wool coat and scarf. His dark hair was slicked back in a way that reminded Gloria of the boys in those 'Wall Street' movies. He reached into the backseat and pulled out two large suitcases before walking up the driveway.

"Danny's here," Gloria said, her voice a mixture of excitement and relief.

Frank smiled. "Told you."

A moment later, the front door opened, and Danny stepped inside, a gust of cold air following him.

"Hey, Mom," he said, setting the suitcases down and pulling off his gloves. "Merry Christmas."

GLORIA RUSHED OVER and enveloped him in a hug, holding him tight. "Merry Christmas, sweetheart. It's so good to have you home."

"Good to be here," Danny replied, though there was a slight hesitation in his voice, as if he was still adjusting to being back in the old house.

Frank stood up and gave his son a firm handshake and a pat on the back. "How's the big city treating you?"

"Busy, as usual," Danny said with a shrug. "But it's good. Work's good."

They made small talk for a few minutes, Gloria asking about the flight, the weather, and how his apartment was. But before long, the sound of another car pulling into the driveway interrupted the conversation.

THIS TIME, it was Mark. He stepped out of a beat-up Volkswagen van, his hair longer than the last time Gloria had seen him, curling at the edges beneath a wool beanie. He wore a leather jacket over a flannel shirt, jeans with holes in the knees, and boots that looked like they'd seen better days. There was a guitar case slung over his shoulder as he walked up to the house.

"Mark!" Gloria exclaimed as he stepped through the door. She wrapped him in a hug, ignoring the cold air that clung to his jacket. "I'm so glad you made it."

"Wouldn't miss it for the world, Mom," Mark said, grinning as he set the guitar down and shook hands with Frank.

"Still touring?" Frank asked, eyeing the guitar.

"Yeah, but I've got a couple weeks off. Figured I'd spend 'em here."

Danny stepped forward and gave his younger brother a nod. "Hey, man. Long time."

"Yeah, it has been," Mark said, his tone more casual than the moment warranted. "How's life in the fast lane?"

"Busy," Danny replied, a little tersely.

Mark just shrugged and smiled. "You always liked it that way."

Gloria felt a pang of tension in the room, a reminder of the sibling rivalry that had always bubbled beneath the surface between her two boys. Danny, the responsible one, had always been driven, focused on his career, while Mark had chosen a more unconventional path, much to Danny's disapproval.

Before the awkward silence could settle, another car pulled into the driveway. This time, it was Sarah, and Gloria's heart lifted at the sight of her baby girl. Sarah stepped out of the car, dressed in a stylish red coat with fur trim, her blonde hair perfectly styled. She looked every bit the successful young woman she had become.

Gloria opened the door before Sarah even reached the porch, pulling her into a warm embrace. "Sarah, sweetheart, you look wonderful."

"Thanks, Mom," Sarah said, smiling as she hugged her mother tightly. "Merry Christmas."

"Merry Christmas," Gloria replied, stepping aside to let her daughter in.

Sarah greeted her father with a hug and her brothers with a smile, though there was a palpable distance between her and Mark. They hadn't been particularly close since they were teenagers, when Sarah's focus on school and Mark's rebellious nature had put them at odds. But it was Christmas, and for now, they all seemed willing to push those old tensions aside.

With everyone finally under one roof, Gloria felt a sense of relief wash over her. The house was filled with the sound of voices, laughter, and the crackle of the fireplace. It was almost like old times.

As the evening wore on, the Taylors gathered in the living room. The Christmas tree twinkled in the corner, and the scent of pine needles mingled with the warmth of the fire. They sat around the coffee table, passing plates of cookies and mugs of hot cocoa, catching up on each other's lives.

Danny talked about his latest projects at the ad agency, the big clients he was landing, and the possibility of a promotion in the new year. Mark shared stories from the road, his band's gigs in cities up and down the East Coast, and his dreams of landing a record deal.

Sarah chimed in with stories from Chicago, where she'd been working her way up in the retail world, managing a department at one of the city's largest stores. She had big plans for the future, too—talk of moving into corporate management, of possibly starting her own business one day.

Gloria listened to it all with a proud smile, though she couldn't shake the feeling that something was missing. Despite the laughter and conversation, there was a distance between her children, a gap that had grown over the years. She wanted to bridge it, to bring them back to the closeness they once had, but she wasn't sure how.

As the night wore on, the conversation began to slow, and the tension that had been simmering beneath the surface finally bubbled over.

It started innocently enough, with Danny making a comment about Mark's music career. "So, how long are you planning to keep playing those little bars? Don't you think it's time to get a real job?"

Mark bristled at the comment, his eyes narrowing. "A real job? Playing music is a real job, Danny. Just because I don't wear a suit and tie every day doesn't mean I'm not working."

Danny leaned back in his chair, arms crossed. "I'm just saying, you're thirty years old. How much longer are you going to keep chasing this dream?"

Mark's voice grew heated. "I'm not chasing anything. I'm doing what I love. Isn't that what matters?"

Sarah, sensing the brewing storm, tried to intervene. "Come on, you two. It's Christmas. Let's not start this."

But the tension had already broken. Danny shook his head. "I just don't get it. You're smart, Mark. You could have done anything with your life, but you chose this. You're wasting your potential."

Mark shot to his feet, fists clenched at his sides. "You always thought you were better than me, didn't you? Just because you've got some fancy job in New York, you think you've got it all figured out. Well, newsflash, Danny—money and status aren't everything."

. . .

DANNY STOOD UP, his voice cold. "At least I'm not a failure."

The words hung in the air, heavy and cutting. Gloria's heart sank. This was exactly what she had feared—that the years apart had built walls between her children that even the warmth of Christmas couldn't break.

Before anyone could say another word, Mark stormed out of the room, grabbing his coat on the way to the door. Sarah looked helplessly between her brothers, then at her parents.

"I'll talk to him," she said softly, following Mark outside.

GLORIA WATCHED from the window as Sarah caught up to Mark on the front porch. They stood in the cold night air, their breath visible in the frigid temperature. Mark's shoulders were hunched, his hands stuffed into his pockets, while Sarah stood with her arms crossed, her face a mixture of concern and frustration.

For a long moment, they just stood there, not speaking. Then, slowly, Sarah reached out and touched Mark's arm. He looked up at her, his expression softening. Whatever words passed between them were lost to the night, but after a moment, Mark nodded, and the two of them walked back toward the house.

WHEN THEY CAME BACK INSIDE, the tension had eased slightly, though the air was still thick with unspoken emotions. Mark sat back down on the couch, and Sarah took a seat beside him.

Danny, who had been standing by the fireplace, sighed and ran a hand through his hair. "I didn't mean what I said," he muttered, his voice barely audible.

Mark glanced at him, then looked away. "Yeah, well... you said it."

There was a long silence before Danny spoke again. "I guess... I just don't understand. I've been so focused on my career, on making a name for myself, that I forgot... that family is important, too."

Mark didn't say anything for a moment, then shrugged. "Yeah. Well, maybe we've both been too focused on ourselves."

Gloria felt a glimmer of hope. It wasn't much, but it was a start.

The rest of the evening passed more quietly, the earlier argument still casting a shadow over the night. But as the fire crackled and the snow fell softly outside, there was a sense that maybe, just maybe, things would be okay. They weren't the same kids who had grown up in this house, running down the stairs on Christmas morning with wide-eyed excitement. They were adults now, with their own lives, their own paths. But no matter how far they had drifted, this house—this family—would always be home.

And in the quiet of the night, as the last embers of the fire glowed softly in the hearth, Gloria Taylor smiled to herself. Because for the first time in a long time, her family was together. And that, more than anything, was what Christmas was all about.

Chapter 9
A Suburban Christmas Eve (1950s)

The crisp December air nipped at the cheeks of children running down maple-lined streets, bundled in woolen scarves and mittens. The sun had dipped behind the horizon early, casting long shadows over rows of identical homes, their pointed roofs capped with fresh snow. It was Christmas Eve in the suburbs, 1956, and the world seemed to glow with anticipation.

THE NEIGHBORHOOD, nestled on the outskirts of a bustling city, was a brand-new development. Rows of freshly built houses with neatly trimmed lawns and white picket fences stretched out as far as the eye could see. Most families had moved in only recently, attracted by the promise of a perfect, quiet life. In a way, it felt like Christmas itself had moved into the suburbs that year, as homes lit up with the soft glow of twinkling lights, and the air filled with the scent of pine, gingerbread, and excitement.

AT THE CENTER of the activity was the Lawrence household, a modest two-story home with green shutters and a large picture window facing the street. Inside, Margaret Lawrence moved about the living room with the energy only a mother on Christmas Eve could muster. Her silver-blonde hair, pinned back in neat curls, shimmered in the soft light from the fireplace. She glanced at the mantle, where garlands of holly interlaced with pinecones had been carefully arranged by her earlier that day, and nodded with satisfaction. Everything was in place.

"Johnny, dear," she called over her shoulder, "Did you find the angel for the top of the tree?"

Her husband, John Lawrence, a tall man with dark hair slicked back like a matinee idol, appeared in the doorway with a triumphant grin. In his hands, he held the delicate porcelain angel, wrapped in tissue paper. "Right where we left it last year," he replied, walking toward the Christmas tree that stood proudly in the corner of the room. The tree was a towering Fraser fir, adorned with tinsel, glass ornaments, and strings of colored lights that blinked in rhythmic patterns.

Their ten-year-old daughter, Evelyn, stood nearby, bouncing on her toes with impatience. Her long brown hair was pulled back into a neat ponytail, and her eyes sparkled with the kind of anticipation only a child could feel on Christmas Eve. "Can I put it on, Daddy?" she asked, holding her arms out for the angel.

John knelt down and placed the angel carefully in her hands. "Of course, sweetheart. But I think you might need a little help getting it all the way up there."

With a quick laugh, he hoisted Evelyn onto his shoulders. Her giggles filled the room as she balanced, reaching up to place the angel on the very top of the tree. Margaret watched them, her hands clasped together, eyes soft with love and pride. It was moments like this that made the chaos of the season worth it.

. . .

OUTSIDE, the sound of distant caroling drifted through the neighborhood. The Lawrence family had always been part of the group that wandered the streets each Christmas Eve, singing to neighbors and spreading cheer. But this year, with the new house, the new neighbors, and the excitement of creating their own traditions, they had decided to host the evening's caroling party in their home. Soon, the neighbors would be arriving for hot chocolate, cookies, and one last round of songs before Santa began his rounds.

MARGARET GLANCED at the clock on the wall—5:45 p.m. "John, could you make sure the record player is ready? And Evelyn, sweetheart, I think it's time to change into your new Christmas dress. The neighbors will be here soon."

Evelyn pouted but did as she was told, bounding up the stairs in search of her new red velvet dress that Margaret had picked out at the department store last week. The dress had satin ribbon at the waist, and Evelyn had insisted it was exactly what Santa's helpers would wear.

As JOHN SET up the record player, spinning a stack of holiday vinyls from Perry Como to Bing Crosby, Margaret moved into the kitchen to check on the batch of cookies she had left cooling on the counter. The smell of ginger and cinnamon filled the air, mingling with the scent of pine from the tree and the sweet warmth of the fire in the hearth. Everything was perfect—just the way it had to be. She glanced out the window and noticed the first of the neighborhood children gathering on the sidewalk, their cheeks rosy from the cold, their voices rising in playful shouts.

. . .

Soon the doorbell rang, and in walked the Thompsons from across the street, followed by the Millers, the Parkers, and a handful of other families from the surrounding blocks. Each group brought something to share—a tin of fudge here, a tray of sugar cookies there—and the Lawrence house quickly became a festive hub of chatter, laughter, and the clinking of mugs filled with hot chocolate and cider.

"Isn't this just lovely?" said Nancy Thompson, a petite woman with curly red hair, as she passed Margaret a tin of homemade peppermint bark. "It feels like we're in one of those stories from the magazines. You know, the ones with the perfect Christmases and perfect houses."

Margaret smiled and nodded. "It does feel magical, doesn't it? Like we've stepped into one of those Norman Rockwell paintings."

John, now standing near the fire, raised a glass of eggnog and called for the attention of the room. "Alright, everyone! Who's ready to start caroling? Let's give this neighborhood a show they'll remember!"

The room erupted in cheers, and within minutes, the crowd spilled out onto the snow-covered sidewalk, scarves and mittens hastily thrown on over holiday dresses and cardigans. Margaret, with her hand wrapped warmly in John's, led the way down the street, their voices rising in unison as they began with "Silent Night," followed by "Deck the Halls" and "O Little Town of Bethlehem."

Evelyn ran ahead, laughing and skipping through the snow with the other children, their feet crunching on the ground as they playfully threw snowballs between verses. The night was still, save for the sound of their voices, and the stars overhead twinkled as though joining in the festivities.

As they rounded the corner onto the next block, the group stopped in front of a house where an older woman stood on her porch, bundled in a thick shawl. Her name was Mrs. Potter, and she had been one of the first people to move into the neighborhood when it was still just a few homes scattered along unpaved roads. Her husband had passed away a few years earlier, and though she kept to herself most of the time, everyone in the neighborhood made sure to check in on her, especially during the holidays.

THE CAROLERS FELL silent as Mrs. Potter waved them closer. "Don't stop on my account," she said with a warm smile. "It's been years since I heard such beautiful singing on Christmas Eve."

John stepped forward, taking off his hat in a polite gesture. "Well, ma'am, we'd be honored to sing for you. How about 'The First Noel'?"

As the group began to sing, Margaret noticed that Mrs. Potter's eyes glistened with unshed tears. There was something about the way the old woman stood on her porch, surrounded by the flickering glow of candles in the windows, that made Margaret's heart ache with a bittersweet kind of nostalgia. It reminded her of her own childhood Christmases, of simpler times when her own parents would gather her close as they stood in their small town square, singing the same carols she sang now.

WHEN THE SONG ENDED, Mrs. Potter clapped her hands together softly. "Thank you," she said, her voice barely above a whisper. "That was just lovely."

The carolers made their way back to the Lawrence house, their voices growing quieter as the cold began to bite a little harder. Once inside, they were greeted by the warmth of the fire and the smell of cocoa simmering on the stove. Margaret handed out mugs, and everyone gathered around the living room, basking in the glow of the tree's lights.

. . .

Evelyn, now seated on the floor by the fire, leaned against her mother's knee. "Momma, do you think Santa's on his way yet?"

Margaret smiled, brushing a strand of hair away from her daughter's face. "I'm sure he's very close, darling. But you'll have to be asleep when he gets here, or he might just pass us by."

Evelyn's eyes grew wide with determination. "I'll go to bed right now, then!"

Everyone in the room chuckled as Evelyn darted off to her room, already shedding her velvet dress on the stairs as she went. John laughed, shaking his head. "That kid. She's been ready for this night all month."

As the evening wore on, the neighbors slowly trickled out, each family exchanging hugs and well-wishes. Margaret stood by the door, thanking each of them for coming and promising they'd do it again next year. The night had gone perfectly, better than she could have imagined. The house, the tree, the laughter—it was the kind of Christmas she had always dreamed of when she was a little girl.

After the last guests had left, John locked the front door and turned to Margaret. "Think we'll ever top this one?"

She smiled up at him, leaning into his warmth. "I don't know if we'll ever need to. I think this one will be perfect in my memory for the rest of my life."

They stood together for a moment, taking in the soft glow of the tree, the quiet hum of the record player still spinning the last few notes of Bing Crosby's "White Christmas." Outside, the world was hushed, as if the whole neighborhood was holding its breath, waiting for morning.

"Come on," John said softly, taking Margaret's hand. "Let's get to bed before Santa beats us to it."

As they climbed the stairs and peeked into Evelyn's room, they found her already fast asleep, clutching her favorite stuffed bear. Her small chest rose and fell softly, her face the picture of contentment, a smile still playing at the corners of her lips.

M‍ARGARET GENTLY CLOSED the door behind them, and as they slipped into their own bed, she found herself whispering a prayer of gratitude for the life they had built, for the little moments that made this Christmas—and all the Christmases to come—so special.

And as the snow continued to fall softly outside, the Lawrence family, like so many others in those postwar suburban enclaves, drifted into a peaceful sleep, the promise of Christmas morning waiting just on the other side of their dreams.

Chapter 10
The Space Age Christmas Tree (1960s)

It was December 1965, and the world was in a dizzying whirl of change. President Kennedy's voice still echoed in the minds of many Americans, speaking of the New Frontier and a vision of landing on the Moon by the end of the decade. Rockets shot into the sky regularly now, their fiery trails visible on TV screens across the nation, as though they were launching from the very living rooms of ordinary families. The future had never felt so near. And yet, as far out as the world seemed to be going, there was still something warm and familiar pulling people back to the roots of home and family—especially at Christmas.

For the Johnston family, Christmas of 1965 was the intersection of these two worlds: the promise of the future and the comfort of tradition. Their home, nestled in a post-war suburb outside of Cincinnati, was filled with the kind of cheer that only came with the holiday season. But this year, their tree was unlike anything they—or anyone else in the neighborhood—had ever had before. It was a Space Age Christmas tree, a gleaming symbol of the times, just as futuristic and dazzling as the space program itself.

A Timeless Christmas: Stories from the 1950s to 1980s

. . .

It had all started when Mary Johnston, the mother and heart of the family, had flipped through the pages of her glossy issue of *Better Homes and Gardens* earlier that month. Her eyes caught on a particular spread featuring a sleek, metallic Christmas tree, glinting with silver tinsel and adorned with geometric ornaments that shimmered like the stars. Above it, perched like the crown jewel of a new, scientific age, was a star topper that glowed with an ethereal blue-white light, as if ready to launch into orbit. Mary was mesmerized.

"Jim," she had said to her husband that evening, "we have to get a tree like this. It's just so... modern!"

Jim, a middle-aged aerospace engineer who worked at the nearby GE plant, had laughed when she showed him the picture. "It looks like something right out of Cape Canaveral, doesn't it?"

"Exactly!" Mary had said, her eyes sparkling. "Wouldn't it be perfect for Christmas this year? What with everything going on in the world, it feels like we're all part of something bigger. Imagine how excited the kids would be!"

Their two children, fourteen-year-old Tommy and ten-year-old Susan, were obsessed with space. Tommy, with his Apollo mission model kits and stacks of *Popular Science* magazines, dreamed of becoming an astronaut one day. Susan, too, was enthralled by the space race, though she was more fascinated with the futuristic possibilities of what people might wear and eat on the Moon.

Jim, always pragmatic, had been hesitant at first. After all, what was wrong with the traditional green tree they'd always had? The same tree they'd been putting up for years, covered in delicate, hand-me-down ornaments from his mother and father, topped with the same angel that had crowned the tree since before he and Mary were even married? It seemed almost sacrilegious to swap out all that history for something so... cold.

But Mary had been persuasive, as always. "It's not just about the tree," she had said, "it's about embracing the future. Our kids will remember this Christmas forever. The world is changing, Jim. And maybe it's time we change with it."

And so, they had gone down to the local department store the following Saturday, where, amidst rows of traditional green firs and colorful glass baubles, stood the tree Mary had seen in the magazine. It was a gleaming aluminum tree, its branches perfectly symmetrical and reflective. It sparkled under the department store's fluorescent lights, almost otherworldly. The salesman had sold them on the "convenience" of it too: no need to water it, no messy pine needles, and best of all, it would last for years.

Jim, though still uncertain, had agreed, and they loaded it into the car. The children, who had been sullen about spending their Saturday shopping, perked up immediately when they saw the futuristic wonder being unpacked in the living room.

"It looks like something out of *Lost in Space!*" Tommy had exclaimed, rushing to help his father assemble it.

Susan, ever the imaginative one, had immediately dubbed it "The Rocket Tree" and danced around the living room, arms extended like she was flying through the stars.

That evening, the family gathered around their new, gleaming centerpiece to decorate it. Instead of the usual colored bulbs and popcorn strings, Mary had found sleek, silver and gold ornaments shaped like stars, rockets, and planets. Some even glowed in the dark, casting an eerie but exciting glow when the lights were turned off.

"Here, put this one near the top," Jim had said, handing Tommy an ornament shaped like Sputnik, the first artificial satellite.

Tommy, who had read everything he could about the Soviet Union's space successes, proudly hung it on the tree's uppermost branch. Susan followed suit, placing a crescent moon ornament just below.

As the final touch, Jim climbed the step ladder to place the tree topper—a glowing, rocket-shaped star—on the highest branch. The star hummed softly as he plugged it in, its light pulsating like the engines of a spacecraft about to take off.

"Perfect!" Mary had declared, stepping back to admire their handiwork. The room was bathed in the tree's silvery glow, and for a moment, they all stood in silence, marveling at the transformation.

"Doesn't it look just like a spaceship, Dad?" Tommy asked, his eyes wide with excitement.

Jim, who had once been so skeptical, found himself smiling. "It sure does, Tommy. It sure does."

A New Kind of Christmas Eve

As Christmas Eve approached, the tree became the center of their holiday activities. Neighbors would drop by, as they often did during the season, curious to see the now infamous "Space Age Christmas tree" they had heard so much about. Some were skeptical, like Jim had been, mumbling about missing the "smell of pine," while others were enchanted, eagerly discussing the possibilities of a future that seemed just around the corner.

Tommy and Susan, of course, were thrilled to show off the tree to their friends. They'd talk about how, someday soon, astronauts might be celebrating Christmas on the Moon or even Mars, exchanging presents in zero gravity, with Christmas trees made from glowing holograms or sleek metal alloys, just like theirs.

. . .

On the night of Christmas Eve, the family gathered around the tree after dinner, just as they always had. Though the tree was new, the traditions were not. Mary brought out the same old tin of homemade cookies, and Jim placed a record of Bing Crosby's "White Christmas" on the turntable, the same song that had filled their home every Christmas since they were married. The children, now older but not so grown that they didn't still believe in some of the Christmas magic, eagerly anticipated the gifts that would be waiting for them the next morning.

But as they sat in the soft glow of the tree's futuristic lights, there was a new kind of excitement in the air—one that blended the wonder of the holiday with the awe of the future. For Tommy and Susan, it wasn't just about what they'd find under the tree anymore. It was about what lay beyond the stars.

"Do you think they'll ever have Christmas on the Moon?" Susan asked, her small voice soft against the crackle of the fire.

Jim, who had spent his days working on the very engines that might one day make such a thing possible, nodded thoughtfully. "Maybe. Someday. It's hard to say exactly when, but it's possible."

Tommy leaned in, eyes wide. "I bet by the time I'm old enough to work at NASA, they'll have colonies up there. And maybe on Mars too! They'll probably decorate with lights that don't need electricity at all. Maybe just sunlight or... or even starlight!"

Mary smiled, watching her children's eyes light up with excitement. It reminded her of the Christmases she had known as a girl, when the world seemed so full of possibility, even after the war. She had never imagined that her own children would be dreaming of such far-off places, places that were once just figments of fantasy, now becoming part of their very real futures.

"You'll have to send us a postcard when you get there," she said with a laugh, though she could see Tommy's face set with determination.

"Oh, I will," he promised. "And I'll bring back a rock for Susan too."

Susan giggled. "I'll probably be living there already. They'll need designers to make space clothes, you know."

Jim chuckled softly. "You two have big plans. But don't forget, Christmas is about more than where you are. It's about family. Whether you're here on Earth or up in the stars, as long as we have each other, it'll always feel like Christmas."

The room fell quiet for a moment, and they all looked toward the tree. The glowing star at the top pulsed gently, its soft light reflecting off the metallic branches, casting tiny pinpoints of light that danced on the walls like the stars in the night sky. It was beautiful in its own strange, modern way—a mix of old warmth and new excitement, a perfect symbol of the times they were living in.

Christmas Morning

The next morning, the family awoke to the soft sound of snow falling outside, its gentle hush blanketing the neighborhood in white. Inside, the tree's metallic sheen contrasted with the softness of the scene, its futuristic glow reminding them all of the world that was changing, even as they clung to the traditions that had always been there.

. . .

Presents were opened, laughter filled the room, and the smells of a holiday breakfast drifted through the air. But more than the gifts, more than the meal, it was the tree that lingered in their memories. For Jim, it was a symbol of a world he was helping to build, a world his children would inherit. For Mary, it was a blend of the new and the old, a sign that, even as the world rushed forward, there was still room for the warmth of home.

For Tommy and Susan, the tree was a promise—a promise that the future was theirs to explore, full of rockets and stars, but also full of the love and comfort that had always been at the heart of Christmas. As they sat by the fire, watching the silver branches twinkle in the light of the morning sun, they knew that this was a Christmas they would never forget.

It was a Christmas that looked toward the future, but cherished the present—a Space Age Christmas, full of hope, dreams, and a tree that shimmered like the stars they would one day reach for.

Closing Thoughts: A Timeless Christmas

As we come to the end of *A Timeless Christmas: Stories from the 1950s to 1980s*, we hope these stories have stirred within you the warmth and wonder of Christmases past. Each tale, set against the backdrop of a different decade, reminds us that while traditions evolve and the world changes, the true spirit of Christmas—love, togetherness, and joy—remains unchanged.

Through tinsel trees, crackling fires, Polaroid snapshots, and department store Santas, these stories reflect not only the holiday season but the passage of time itself. They are a tribute to the small moments that linger in our hearts long after the gifts are unwrapped and the decorations are taken down.

Whether these stories brought back your own memories or painted a picture of an era you've never known, they serve as a reminder of how deeply the holidays connect us. No matter where we come from or how we celebrate, Christmas is a time to reflect on what matters most: family, love, and the timeless joy of giving and sharing.

As you close this book and return to your own holiday traditions, we invite you to carry forward the nostalgia, the warmth, and the

Closing Thoughts: A Timeless Christmas

magic of these stories into your own celebrations. May your Christmases—past, present, and future—be filled with love, laughter, and the enduring spirit of the season.

Thank you for joining us on this journey through time. Merry Christmas, and may the joy of the season stay with you always.

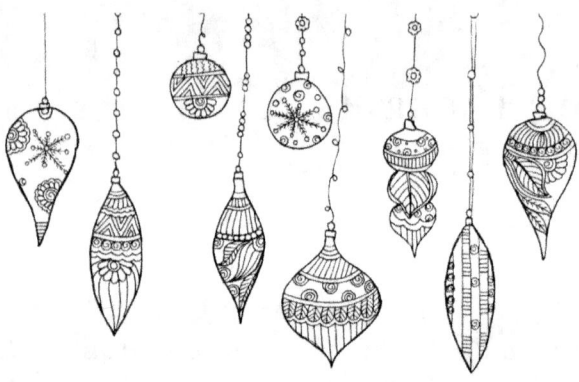

www.ingramcontent.com/pod-product-compliance
Lightning Source LLC
LaVergne TN
LVHW012126070526
838202LV00056B/5885